FiVE LiTTLE GEFiLTES

dave horowitz   G. P. Putnam's Sons

ACKNOWLEDGMENTS

My mother likes to say, "As the pot stinks, so stinks the broth."

It's the Yiddish way of saying . . . well, I don't know what exactly.

So here's to everyone who helped make this book stink so good.

First, to my grandmother, "Mommy Frieda" Pakulsky, for her tireless humor and support of this book.

To my editor, Nancy Paulsen, who, despite her dislike of real gefilte fish,

provided enthusiasm and guidance from the beginning.

To Cecilia Yung and Gina DiMassi, my design-mishpucha—simply the best.

And of course to my parents, who always taught me, above everything, to be a mensch.

G. P. PUTNAM'S SONS A division of Penguin Young Readers Group. Published by The Penguin Group. Penguin Group (USA) Inc., 375 Hudson Street, New York, NY 10014, U.S.A. Penguin Group (Canada), 90 Eglinton Avenue East, Suite 700, Toronto, Ontario, Canada M4P 2Y3 (a division of Pearson Penguin Canada Inc.). Penguin Books Ltd, 80 Strand, London WC2R 0RL, England. Penguin Ireland, 25 St. Stephen's Green, Dublin 2, Ireland (a division of Penguin Books Ltd.). Penguin Group (Australia), 250 Camberwell Road, Camberwell, Victoria 3124, Australia (a division of Pearson Australia Group Pty Ltd). Penguin Books India Pvt Ltd, 11 Community Centre, Panchsheel Park, New Delhi - 110 017, India. Penguin Group (NZ), Cnr Airborne and Rosedale Roads, Albany, Auckland 1310, New Zealand (a division of Pearson New Zealand Ltd). Penguin Books (South Africa) (Pty) Ltd, 24 Sturdee Avenue, Rosebank, Johannesburg 2196, South Africa. Penguin Books Ltd, Registered Offices: 80 Strand, London WC2R 0RL, England.

Published simultaneously in Canada. Manufactured in China. Design by Gina DiMassi. Text set in Kane. The art was done with cut paper, charcoal and colored pencils. Library of Congress Cataloging-in-Publication Data Horowitz, Dave, 1970–   Five little gefiltes / Dave Horowitz. p.   cm.   Summary: Five little gefilte fish sneak out of their jar and explore the world, causing their poor mother great worry. Includes a note about gefilte fish and a glossary of Yiddish words. [1. Counting. 2. Humorous stories. 3. Stories in rhyme.] I. Title. PZ8.3.H7848Fi 2007 [E]—dc22   2006011909 ISBN 978-0-399-24608-1

for Poppy

Sam "Poppy" Pakulsky (third from right) in 1920, just before crossing the great ocean with his siblings.

What's a Gefilte?

Gefilte fish is a traditional food popular with Jewish people all over the world. But don't go looking in the ocean for a gefilte fish . . .

Regular fish →

← Gefilte fish

Gefilte fish are balls made from several different
kinds of fish—pike, carp and whitefish, to name a few.
They're like matzo balls made out of fish.

Feh!
that's
disgusting—

So who's asking you to eat one? . . .
Now, on with our story.

FIVE little gefiltes went out one day,
out of the jar and far away.

Mama Gefilte
cried out

OY VeY!

but only four little gefiltes
came back that day.

FOUR little gefiltes
went out one day.
They went to the theater
and took in a play.

Mama Gefilte
cried out

Oy Vey!

but only three little gefiltes
came back that day.

THREE little gefiltes went out one day.
They went for a swim in the great New York Bay.

Vey!

but only two little gefiltes
came back that day.

Mama Gefilte
cried out

OY VeY!

but only one little gefilte
came back that day.

ONE little gefilte went out one day.
A big yellow taxi shlepped him away.

Mama Gefilte
cried out

Vey!

but not a single gefilte
came back that day.

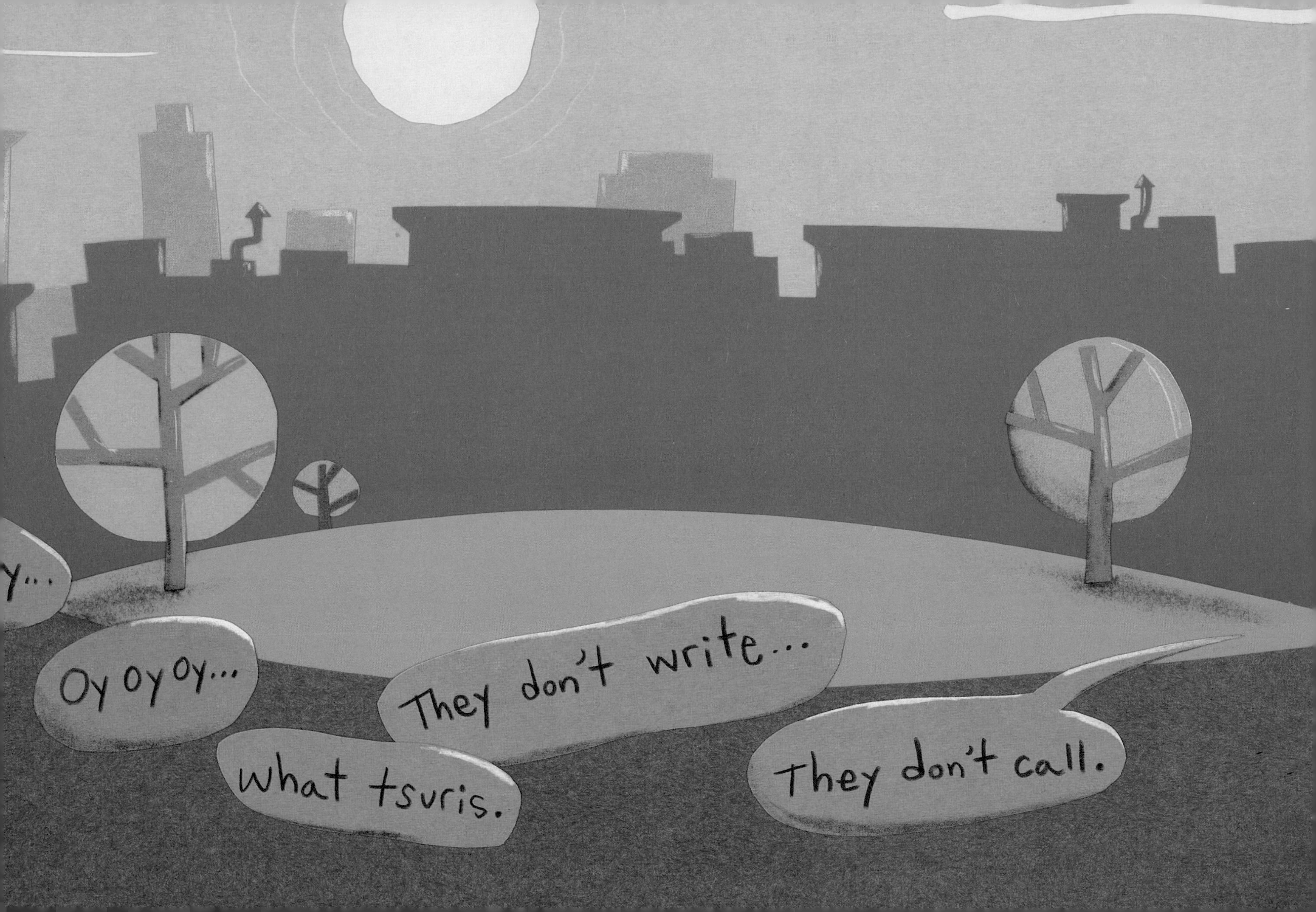
y...
Oy oy oy...
What tsuris.
They don't write...
They don't call.

Sad Mama Gefilte went out one day.
She went to the park and
kvetched the whole way.

She finally got tired and sat on a bench . . .

And the gefiltes came back
'cause each was a mensch!

What's a Mensch?
(and other meshugana words from this book)

BUBBE (BUB-ee) noun: Grandmother.

CHAZA (KHA-za) noun: A pig or a glutton.

a chaza

CHUTZPAH (KHOOTS-pa) noun: Nerve. Bravado. *Example: Dave got someone to publish this ridiculous book about a bunch of gefilte fish? Now that's what I call chutzpah!*

FEH (F'EH) interjection: Yuck!

GEFILTE FISH (ga-FILL-ta FISH) noun: Well, if you don't know by now . . .

KNISH (ka-NISH) noun: A pastry usually filled with potato.

KREPLACH (CREP-lokh) noun: A tasty fried dumpling. Like a Jewish wonton.

KVELL (KVELL) verb: To beam proudly.

KVETCH (k-VETCH) verb: To complain.

LOX (LOCKS) noun: Smoked salmon.

MATZO (MAHT-tsa) noun: Unleavened bread.

MATZO BALL (MAHT-tsa BALL) noun: A ball made from matzo and eggs, typically served in soup. Like a gefilte fish without all the fish.

MENSCH (MENTCH) noun: A morally good person. *Example: My mother always says the most important thing in life is to be a mensch.*

MESHUGANA (muh-SHUG-a-nah) adjective: Crazy.

MISHPUCHA (meesh-PUKH-ah) noun: Family.

NOSH (NOSH) noun/verb: A little something to eat/to eat a little something.

OY VEY (OY VEY) interjection: The most useful term in the Yiddish language, *oy vey* can mean anything from "holy cow" to "oh my" to "you gotta be kidding me."

PLOTZ (PLOTS) verb: To collapse in shock.

SHLEP (SHLEP) verb: To carry or drag.

S'GUT (suh'GOOT) adjective: So good.

SHMATA (SHMA-tah) noun: A rag.

SHMALTZ (SHMALTZ) noun: Chicken fat used for cooking (feh).

SHMEAR (SHMEER) noun: A little bit of something. Usually spreadable. *Example: Do you want cream cheese on that bagel? Okay—but just a shmear.*

SHNOOK (SHNOOK) noun: Fool.

a shnook

SHVITZ (SHVITS) verb: To sweat.

TSURIS (TSOO-ris) noun: Troubles.

TUCHES (TUKH-is) noun: Tushy.

WADDAYA TALKIN' . . . ? (WAHD-ah-ya TALK-ing?) phrase: What are you talking about?

YIDDISH (YID-ish) noun: The language and culture of the Eastern European Jews. Like this book, Yiddish is often quite meshugana, wouldn't you say?